Layla   Jayden   Caleb

They are Kid Force 3.

THE TOXIC COOKIE MONSTER

TONY BRADMAN   WIL OVERTON

EDGE
FRANKLIN WATTS
W

LONDON·SYDNEY

Franklin Watts
First published in Great Britain in 2018 by The Watts Publishing Group

Executive Editor: Adrian Cole
Design Manager: Peter Scoulding
Cover Designer: Cathryn Gilbert
Illustrations: Wil Overton

HB ISBN 978 1 4451 5634 7
PB ISBN 978 1 4451 5635 4
Library ebook ISBN 978 1 4451 6201 0

Printed in China

MIX
Paper from
responsible sources
FSC
www.fsc.org   FSC® C104740

Franklin Watts
An imprint of
Hachette Children's Group
Part of The Watts Publishing Group
Carmelite House
50 Victoria Embankment
London EC4Y 0DZ

An Hachette UK Company
www.hachette.co.uk

www.franklinwatts.co.uk

7

8

9

"Mrs Fox does love cookies," said Layla.

"Why did she jump out of the window?" asked Jayden.

"Maybe she's really, really hungry,"
said Layla.

"Wait! Look at these cookies," said Caleb.

12

"Wow! What happened to Mrs Fox?" asked Layla.

"The toxic cookies are making her grow. That's why she needs to keep eating," said Caleb.

"When will she stop?" asked Jayden.

"She won't," replied Caleb.

"I can build a machine. It will change her back," said Caleb.

"We can help," said Layla and Jayden.

"We will need a lot of energy," said Caleb.

"I can supply that," replied Jayden.

"And a lot of cookies," added Caleb.

"I can get those," replied Layla.

24

25

28

30